The Ant Picnic

by David Webb
illustrated by Dave Blanchette

Printed in the United States of America

ISBN 0-15-317191-X – The Ant's Picnic

Ordering Options
ISBN 0-15-318578-3 (Package of 5)
ISBN 0-15-316985-0 (Grade 1 Package)

3 4 5 6 7 8 9 10 179 02 01 00

Look at me!
What do you see?

I'm so small.
Do you see me at all?

2

My friends are small, too.
They are looking at you!

We are digging in a log.
So we can pass the big dog.

4

Down we all go.
We come up—oh!

What do I see?
I see cookies for me!

"Look! It's a snack!" I call.
I toss the cookies to one
and all.

Oh, what a happy day
for me.
I saw my friends and
they saw me!

Teacher/Family Member ....

Ant Antics
Sing a song about ants, such as "The Ants Go Marching." Encourage children to act out the song or add finger movements to show the actions of the ants.

 School-Home Connection
Ask your child to read *The Ant's Picnic* to you. Then help your child find the pairs of rhyming words in the story. Have him or her think of other words that rhyme with each pair.

Word Count: 85

Vocabulary Words:
I'm	oh
so	day
friends	saw
they	

Phonic Elements:
Consonant: /g/*g*
digging	dog
log	go
big	

Double consonant: /s/*ss*
pass	toss

Inflection: *-ing* (double final consonant)
digging

TAKE-HOME BOOK
You're Invited
Use with "Lost!" and "What Day Is It?"